Shark in the Dark!

Nick Sharratt

PICTURE CORGI

Just before bedtime,
a certain small boy
stands at the window
with his favourite toy.

Timothy Pope, Timothy Pope
is looking through his telescope.

He looks at the sky
and the moon up there.

He looks left.

He looks right.

He looks
everywhere.

And this
is what he sees.

Jumping jellyfish!
What's that bobbing in the dark?
Could it be a

GREAT

WHITE

SHARK?

A shark?
No it's not.
It's the sail on
a yacht!

Timothy Pope, Timothy Pope
looks again through his telescope.

He looks at the sky
and the moon up there.

He looks left.

He looks right.

He looks
everywhere.

And this
is what he sees.

Stumbling starfish!

What's that swishing through the dark?
Could it be a

GREAT

WHITE

SHARK?

It's a seagull with his tea!"

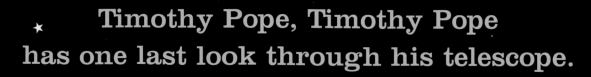

Timothy Pope, Timothy Pope
has one last look through his telescope.

He looks at the sky
and the moon up there.

He looks left.

He looks right.

He looks
everywhere.

And this
is what he sees.

Quivering catfish!
What's that lurking in the dark?
Could it be a

GREAT
WHITE
SHARK?

Don't worry Tim,
there's no need to scream.

It isn't a shark,
it's a giant
ice cream!

Tim says to his dad,
"I'm sure I'm right.
There are no sharks
in the dark tonight."